No Clean Clothes

No Clean Clothes

Robert Munsch

illustrated by
Michael Martchenko

SCHOLASTIC CANADA LTD.

New York Toronto London Auckland Sydney
Mexico City New Delhi Hong Kong Buenos Aires

Scholastic Canada Ltd.
604 King Street West, Toronto, Ontario M5V 1E1, Canada

Scholastic Inc.
557 Broadway, New York, NY 10012, USA

Scholastic Australia Pty Limited
PO Box 579, Gosford, NSW 2250, Australia

Scholastic New Zealand Limited
Private Bag 94407, Greenmount, Auckland, New Zealand

Scholastic Children's Books
Euston House, 24 Eversholt Street, London NW1 1DB, UK

The illustrations in this book were painted in watercolour on Crescent illustration board.
The type is set in 21 point Plantin.

Library and Archives Canada Cataloguing in Publication
Munsch, Robert N., 1945-

No clean clothes / Robert Munsch ; illustrated by Michael Martchenko.
ISBN 0-439-93790-6

I. Martchenko, Michael II. Title.
PS8576.U575N6 2006a   jC813'.54   C2006-902367-0

ISBN-10 0-439-93790-6 / ISBN-13 978-0-439-93790-0

6 5   Printed in Canada   07 08 09 10

To Lacey Clarke
Stewart, British Columbia.
— R.M.

Lacey opened the top drawer of her dresser:

NO CLEAN CLOTHES!

Lacey opened the middle drawer of her dresser:

NO CLEAN CLOTHES!

Lacey opened the bottom drawer of her dresser:

NO CLEAN CLOTHES!

Lacey looked all around her bedroom: NO CLEAN CLOTHES!

She ran downstairs and yelled, "Mom! Mom! Mom! Why didn't you wash my clothes?"

"Lacey," said her mother, "I would WASH your clothes if I could FIND your clothes!

"You hide them under your bed!

"You lend them to your friends!

"You leave them in the backyard!

"Sometimes I think you feed your underwear to the dog!"

"Mom," said Lacey, "don't be silly! All I need is one shirt. Can't you find me just one clean shirt?"

"Well," said her mom, "there is that nice shirt that Grandma gave you for your birthday. You have never worn it."

"That shirt is a Strange Grandma Present," said Lacey.

"When I was three, Grandma gave me a shirt that said SNOOGIE WOOKUMS, and everyone laughed at me.

"When I was four, Grandma gave me a shirt that said CUTIE PATOOTIE, and everyone laughed at me."

"When I was five, Grandma gave me a shirt that said CUDDLY WUNKUMS, and everyone laughed at me.

"Now I am six, and Grandma gives me a shirt that says KISS ME — I'M PERFECT. I am NOT wearing that shirt to school. Only a grandma would choose a shirt like that."

"Now Lacey," said her mom, "just wear it for this morning. I will wash a shirt and bring it to school at recess."

"You will wash it right away?" said Lacey.

"Yes," said Lacey's mom.

"You will not talk on the phone?"

"No," said her mom.

"You will not wash the dishes?"

"No," said her mom.

"You will not go shopping on the way?"

"No," said her mom.

"You will not go to work and chop down a tree?"

"No," said her mom.

"OK!" said Lacey. "I will be on the steps of the school at recess."

Lacey put on the Strange Grandma Shirt and walked down the road. A kitty cat looked up at her, read her shirt, and gave her a kitty cat kiss on her ear:

Lick — Lick — Lick — Lick — Lick — Lick

"Neat!" said Lacey. "I got a kitty-cat kiss. Maybe I am going to like this shirt."

She walked farther down the street and met a dog.

The dog read Lacey's shirt, jumped up, and gave her a doggy kiss on the ear:

Sphlick — Sphlick — Sphlick

"WOW!" said Lacey. "I got a kitty-cat kiss and a doggy kiss! This is a wonderful shirt!"

Lacey walked farther down the street. An eagle flew in circles around her and landed on her head. It leaned down, read her shirt, and gave her an eagle kiss on the nose:

DINK — DINK — DINK

Lacey yelled, "An eagle kiss! An eagle kiss! I got an eagle kiss! I love my grandma! I love this shirt!"

Lacey walked farther down
the street and met a moose.

The moose looked at Lacey, read her shirt, and gave her a large wet moose kiss right up the front of her face and over the top of her head:

SPHLURRRRRRRRRRRRCHHHHH

"Fantastic!" said Lacey. "I am the first person ever to be kissed by a moose."

When Lacey got to school, she ran inside and yelled, "Teacher! Teacher! Look! I got a kitty-cat kiss. I got a doggy kiss. I got an eagle kiss. I got a moose kiss — all because of my Wonderful Grandma Shirt!"

"Neat," said her teacher. "But maybe you should go and wash. Your hair is full of green moose slime."

"Yuck!" said Lacey. "Very gross!"

When Lacey came back to her desk, a boy named Johnny sat down beside her. He read her shirt and gave her a kiss.

"GWAAAAACHHHHK!" yelled Lacey.

"BOY KISS! AHHHHHHH!" She ran back into the bathroom and washed her face until recess. Then she went back outside and got really lucky because she was kissed . . .

BY A BEAR!

When Lacey got home after school her mother said, "I didn't see you at school. Did Grandma's shirt turn out to be OK?"

"I love it," said Lacey. "And I called Grandma from the principal's office. She's going to send everyone at school a Strange Grandma Shirt."